RUBY ALI'S MISSION BREAK UP

SUFIYA AHMED

ILLUSTRATED BY
PARWINDER SINGH

BLOOMSBURY EDUCATION
LONDON OXFORD NEW YORK NEW DELHI SYDNEY

BLOOMSBURY EDUCATION

Bloomsbury Publishing Plc
50 Bedford Square, London, WC1B 3DP, UK
29 Earlsfort Terrace, Dublin 2, Ireland

BLOOMSBURY, BLOOMSBURY EDUCATION and the Diana logo are trademarks of
Bloomsbury Publishing Plc

First published in Great Britain in 2021 by Bloomsbury Publishing Plc

Text copyright © Sufiya Ahmed, 2021
Illustrations copyright © Parwinder Singh, 2021

Sufiya Ahmed and Parwinder Singh have asserted their rights under the Copyright,
Designs and Patents Act, 1988, to be identified as Author and Illustrator
of this work

A catalogue record for this book is available from the British Library

ISBN: PB: 978-1-4729-9317-5; ePDF: 978-1-4729-9316-8; ePub: 978-1-4729-9315-1

2 4 6 8 10 9 7 5 3 1

Printed and bound in in the UK by CPI Group Ltd, CR0 4YY

To find out more about our authors and books visit www.bloomsbury.com and sign up
for our newsletters

CONTENTS

The Break Up   7

New Beginnings   17

Operation Odd Socks   25

Operation Glue   35

Creepy Crawlies   45

The Surprise Prankster   51

Pizzagate   57

Sweet Bowl of Mash   65

Smashed Screen   71

Another Mission   83

THE BREAK UP

"Why can't I come with you?" I mumble, clutching my old stuffed rabbit, Bug, to my chest.

My sister Alisha's head shoots up from the bin bag she's packing.

"Ruby!" she snaps. "We've been through this. You repeating yourself isn't going to change the fact that you can't be with me. We have to go our separate ways. You'll get fostered by a good family who like little girls. You're only twelve. This is the best thing for you."

"I…"

She cuts me off. "And don't you think you're a little old for Bug now?"

My mouth falls open. How could she say that? She knows what Bug means to me. Alisha looks like she wants to add something more, but she changes her mind and looks away. Perhaps the hurt on my face is too obvious. Her lips press together in a straight line and she busies herself with her packing again. I can tell she's upset because she's stuffing her clothes in, rather than folding them neatly. Neither of us have many belongings as the care system only pays for our essentials.

I am finding it hard to accept that she is separating from me. Now that she's eighteen, Alisha's not allowed to stay in care anymore. She's going to move in with her new friend, Julie, who rents a house with five others at an address which I've secretly memorised.

It also means she is leaving me behind. I stare down at her as she shoves the last of her clothes into her bin bag. Her silky long black hair falls forward like a curtain, half concealing her face as she presses down on the load so that she can tie a knot at the top. Strangers have always said that she's an older version of me. The only difference, these days, is the make-up caked on her face. Black kohl rims her brown eyes, and her lipstick is a plum shade. When she first wore the colour, I told her she looked like she'd eaten blackberries.

"Julie likes it," had been her reply.

I'd rolled my eyes. Of course, Julie would like it. She is a goth, after all. Oh, how I hate her influence on my sister's life. With the knot securely tied, Alisha gets to her feet. Is this it? My heart begins to beat frantically in my chest.

She is leaving.

She is really leaving me.

I lunge forward to throw my arms around her waist. I am terrified to be without her. I've never been without her.

"You promised we would always be together!" I wail.

"And we were together," she says softly, recognising my panic. Her earlier impatience is no more, and she tries to soothe me. Ever so gently, she unwraps my arms from her middle and holds my hands. "Rubes, I need to make my own way in the world. I can't take you. Please understand. It isn't allowed."

I look up at her pleadingly. "When have you ever followed the rules?"

She drops my hands. "How many times must I explain it to you? The system won't pay me to look after you. I'm not a foster carer."

"What if nobody else in the world wanted me?" I ask. "Would they let you have me then?"

"Yes, well maybe," she says vaguely, glancing at the white clock on the wall.

I say nothing as she places a kiss on my forehead. I can tell she is feeling emotional too. How can she not be?

"I'll come and see you as soon as I'm settled," she promises. "And in a year or two, you can move in with me when I have a good job and flat." Then, without giving me a chance to say anything, she picks up her bin bag and walks out of the door without turning back even once.

I stare at the white door with the big poster of fire instructions nailed to the centre. I know the list of what to do in the event of fire by heart, but I re-read it anyway. The focus helps me swallow the lump that has formed in my throat. I can't allow myself to cry. If I do, it will be the first time Alisha won't be with me to wipe my tears. And I am terrified of crying on my own.

After taking several deep breaths to control the butterflies zooming around in my tummy, I turn to the window and wait for her to appear below. Alisha takes her time to emerge out of the big Georgian house that is the residential home for children. It is called Sunshine House. I imagine she is saying goodbye to the workers in the office. We, the Ali sisters, have been in and out of Sunshine House for years. Somehow, our time with foster families never seemed to last very long. Our last foster stay ended two weeks ago because Alisha hated it and we've been living here since.

I glance at my own bin bag, packed and knotted to take with me to my new foster home. The thought of living with strangers without Alisha fills me with dread. For comfort, I bury my face in my rabbit. The fur is matted and stained with dirt, but I don't care. Bug was the last thing Mum gave me. When he lost his right ear, I promised myself that Bug would never end up in the hot spin of Claire's horror machine ever again. Or anyone else's for that matter. I remember that day well. I was nine years old, and it is scarred into my memory.

"Please not Bug," I pleaded.

I was no match for Claire's big strong hands.

11

"It's dirty!" she insisted, furiously grabbing Bug from me. "Rabia!"

She was the only foster we'd ever had who insisted on calling me by my full name, even after I'd told her loads of times that I preferred to be called Ruby.

That day, poor Bug had not only lost his ear, but Mum's scent, which had lingered on it for years. Alisha tried to comfort me by saying that the scent had evaporated a long time ago.

"It's gone, Rubes, just like Mum."

I hadn't agreed. It had been the first time I'd thrown a tantrum. I had screamed, thrown objects and refused to eat for days until our social worker was summoned. That was Poonam, who affectionately introduced herself as Poo to every child. I think it was to make the bewildered, scared children relax and laugh. I'd certainly giggled when she'd lifted me as a six-year-old into her arms for the first time and said, "Hello, I'm Poo."

Poo hadn't been too pleased when she had picked us up from Claire's home to return us to Sunshine House. "I'd expected that behaviour from Alisha," she'd admonished in the car. "Not you, Ruby."

"I told Claire I didn't want Bug to go in the washing machine," I said tearfully. "She didn't listen to me and now Bug's lost his ear."

Poo's voice softened. "Did you rescue his ear from the machine?"

I nodded. "It's in my pocket."

"I'll sew it back on for you when we get back to Sunshine House," Poo offered. "And then Bug will be just like before."

"What about Mum's smell?"

Poo had no comeback for that.

"That Claire only takes in kids so she can scrub them clean," Alisha said. "She was always shouting at me for the littlest things like mud on my boots or rainwater dripping off the umbrella in the hallway."

"And I suppose you never played any pranks on her, angel that you are?" Poo said in a sarcastic voice.

Alisha met Poo's eyes in the rear-view mirror and widened them innocently. "Who, me?"

Poo tutted. She knew us better than anyone else in the world.

* * *

Alisha finally appears outside. She doesn't look up, even though she must know that I'm standing there to wave a final goodbye.

I have spent the last six years of my life looking out of windows and standing by doors waiting for my big sister after school. The difference this time, though, is that she isn't coming home to me, but rather walking away from me. It's not her fault. I can see that now. It is the system that forbids us to be together. It is the system that must be beaten.

And so, as she walks away for the final time from Sunshine House, the plan to break away from my next foster family forms in my mind: Mission Break Up.

NEW BEGINNINGS

Poo pulls her car up outside Number 65 Drummond Street. The house is semi-detached with a drive big enough for two cars, although only one is parked on it. The front is painted a pastel colour, just like the other houses on this road. This one is green, and there is a mixture of pink, yellow, blue and purple. The entire line-up reminds me of a packet of fruit pastilles.

"This is it," Poo says, turning in her seat to face me.

I have known Poo now for as long as I knew my mum. Six years, and in all this time she has hardly changed. She still wears colourful, patterned dresses over skinny jeans and converse trainers. I think she has all the colours of converses you can buy because she can match the colour to her dress on most days.

Today her converses are red to go with her poppy patterned dress.

All the children attached to Sunshine House adore Poo. She is like a fun aunt with her casual clothes, bright red lipstick and short brown hair.

"Ruby," Poo says gently, "this is a new chance for you to make a new home."

I say nothing.

Her mouth sets in a straight line. "You're no longer in Alisha's shadow. She's not here to cause chaos."

I shrug. "Whatever."

"I mean it, Ruby," Poo's voice is suddenly firm. "No pranks. No tantrums. If you mess this one up, I'll really struggle to find someone else to take you on."

I lower my head to hide the small smile on my lips.

Within the next five minutes, we are sitting in the living room of the big house.

I gaze at my new foster carer, Cheryl. She looks to be about thirty-five and has short brown hair and brown eyes. Her husband, Jim, looks a little older and has the same colouring. They are both dressed in jeans and t-shirts.

These fosters look like kind people, the type whose smiles are warm and friendly. They even have lots of those little lines around their eyes, which must mean they spend a lot of time laughing. Poo told me in the car that they were experienced carers. They had fostered babies and toddlers before, all of whom had gone on to be adopted.

When I was six and adorably cute, Poo had tried really hard to have me adopted. There had been interest from several couples, but Alisha was having none of it, and she instructed me to be as disgusting as possible to put them off. I had talked with my mouth full of food, peed in my knickers, stomped my feet and screamed when I was greeted with a hello. I became the opposite of the little angelic girl in my care plan photo. The one with the cute oval face, big brown eyes and pigtails. The interest soon fell away. In the end, some little babies came into care and the couples jumped at the chance to raise brand-new humans, instead of horrid little girls like me.

Of course, I wasn't normally disgusting. It was an act so I could stay with Alisha. She had promised we would never be separated. Well, she'd broken that promise now, and here I was sitting in awkward silence with Poo and two strangers.

"Would you like to see your room?" Cheryl asks.

"Yes, Mrs Brown, I would like to see my room," I reply on cue.

She flashes perfect white teeth at me. "Oh, you don't have to call me that. Cheryl will do."

"No formalities in this house," Jim adds.

Gosh, I hope they're not the free-living type who like to go litter-picking at the weekend and refuse to have any plastic in the house. Alisha and I have experience of those type of fosters too. Predictably, our stay didn't last long. Alisha made sure of it by buying cling film from the pound shop and wrapping it around all the food in the fridge. She called it our right to protest litter-picking-forced-labour. Poo had pretended to be furious when she'd arrived to pick us up, and then laughed in the car all the way back to Sunshine House.

Poo is not laughing right now. She looks deadly serious as she stands up. "Right, I shall leave you all to it. You have the numbers for emergencies."

"We do," Jim says. "Thank you, Poonam."

Poo turns to me and I can see the concern in her eyes. "Be a good girl, Ruby. This is a lovely home and Jim and Cheryl are really pleased to be looking after you."

"Thank you, Poo," I manage in a dull voice. I just can't muster up fake enthusiasm. It was always Alisha who did the talking. I only ever had to stand behind her.

The dread in my chest is heavy as I watch the last familiar face I know drive away. I'm here now with strangers and I must start all over again with my new "family". Alone.

"Let's go to your room," Cheryl says.

I nod and follow her up the stairs. Jim remains in the living room.

My bedroom is large and cheery with yellow stripey wallpaper and big windows that add light. There is a big bed, double wardrobe and a dressing table. There are even some books on the shelf. I do enjoy reading and look forward to going through them.

Cheryl hovers near the door. "Would you like a hand unpacking?"

"I'm fine, thank you."

"Are you sure?"

"I'm fine," I mumble. "I don't have many things to unpack."

"Hazard of always moving around, I suppose," Cheryl says.

I give her my you-really-said-it look. Yes, it's true that foster kids move around a lot, but there's no need to rub it in.

I think she gets the meaning of my look because she suddenly looks flustered. "Right, I'll be in the kitchen," she says. "Come down when you're ready. I've made a delicious meat lasagne."

I bite my lip. So, she has not even read my care plan.

"I'm quite tired," I say. "Would you please leave a tray outside for me?"

"A tray?"

"A cheese sandwich and a glass of milk."

Cheryl looks like she wants to object, thinks better of it, and then closes the door behind her. I collapse on the bed to stare up at the ceiling. Gold and silver stars glitter down at me. They were probably glued on for the younger children fostered before. I count ten stars in total and then sigh heavily at my situation.

Joining new fosters in the summer holidays is the worst thing ever. It means that I'll be forced to spend most of the time with them. Alisha and I once lived with a couple who wanted us to read books, watch documentaries on Netflix and even cook together. It had all been too much. Alisha had resisted and kept us locked in our rooms. That had been fine because we'd had each other's company.

Being holed up on my own here is going to be very different. To tell the truth, I imagine it is going to be really, really lonely. Then my eyes fall on the bookshelf. I get up to see the covers. Well, at least I'll have the stories for company until I can execute Mission Break Up.

OPERATION ODD SOCKS

My hair is a complete mess.

It is so long and there is so much of it. Washing it takes ages as does drying and detangling it. I slam the comb down on the dresser and scowl at myself in the mirror. Alisha always combed my hair after it was washed.

And now I am having to do it myself!

I think about just tying it back and leaving the detangling for another day.

"Ruby?"

I glance over my shoulder. Cheryl is standing by the open door.

"Can I come in?" she asks.

I shrug.

She perches on my bed. "You have lovely hair," she says. "Long and thick. What I wouldn't do for it."

"It's Asian hair," I say. "We all have hair like this."

Cheryl leans forward. "You haven't combed it properly. There are still knots."

I shrug again.

"Would you like me to comb it?"

I look up in surprise. I don't know how I feel about that. Alisha never allowed anyone else to come near me. Ever. She had done all the caring for me herself. But she isn't here now.

A part of me wants Cheryl to help with my hair, but another part wants to keep her at a distance. After all, the mission is to break with the fosters. I can't let Cheryl's niceness confuse me and stop me from achieving Mission Break Up.

"No, I'm fine."

A disappointed sound escapes her. I can tell I've hurt her with my flippant refusal. Well, it can't be helped. She should be looking after babies and toddlers who need care, not separating twelve-year-old girls like me from their flesh and blood.

Cheryl gets up to leave. "I just remembered I've got some washing to put out."

I stare at my face in the mirror when I'm alone again. What am I to do? I can't let Cheryl touch me, but I can't comb my hair either.

There is only one solution.

I go down to the kitchen for a pair of scissors. Finding some big silver ones in Cheryl's sewing basket, I return to my room and sit straight-backed in front of the mirror.

This is it.

Taking a deep breath, I begin to chop.

Chop.

Chop.

Soon, long strands cover the grey carpet around my feet. I snip a bit more here and there. My new hairstyle is a jagged cut around my shoulders. It looks terrible but I feel relief. I won't have to worry about my hair anymore.

That evening, I go down to dinner with my hair in a small ponytail. Cheryl stares at me in shock.

"Your hair," she mumbles.

"I like it short," I say with a shrug.

"It doesn't look very even," Jim says, peering at me before turning to Cheryl. "Why don't you take Ruby to the hairdressers tomorrow?"

Cheryl nods. "Would you like that? Sandy, my hairdresser, could tidy it for you."

I don't have to think about it. I don't want the fosters to do anything for me. It would distract me from Mission Break Up. "No."

Cheryl's face falls, but she doesn't say anything.

"What's for dinner?" Jim asks, changing the subject.

"Pesto pasta," Cheryl replies.

The vegetarian dish is the reason I've agreed to come down. I wolf my plate down and eat extra amounts even though my tummy is full. Alisha taught me to stow away food like a hibernating animal in case our next meal was delayed. I notice Cheryl eyeing me with concern.

"Hungry today," she says.

I nod, mouth full, and sneak a peek at Jim from under my lashes. I observe him and try to work out how far I can go with my first prank in Mission Break Up.

Alisha always taught me that it was wise to test the waters first in case the foster dad had a horrid temper. It meant starting with small rebel moves to gauge the reaction.

"Some people," she would say, "are wired to lose control completely."

I knew she was referring to Dad at these times. And now Mum is gone, and Dad isn't allowed to see us.

I don't really remember him. Alisha does, though, and with lots of hatred too.

I give my head a slight shake to forget the past and focus on the present. Earlier this evening, I made a list of pranks and ordered them from cool pink to red hot.

The first on the list is Operation Sock Drawer. Alisha played this one on Claire. Typically, she had gone bananas and ordered Alisha to rematch every pair. Then she had refused to serve Alisha dinner that night. Poo had not been very impressed when we'd told her. I think Poo removed Claire from the foster-carer list after our stay.

It's time to put my plan into action.

I wonder how Jim and Cheryl will react as I

tiptoe out into the hallway. They are in the living room watching TV.

I pause outside their bedroom and take a deep breath. This is it. I am about to break one of the top ten rules of care. No foster child is allowed to enter a foster's bedroom without permission. But I'm about to do it to for the sake of Mission Break Up.

Opening their door, I head to the dresser. The socks are in the third drawer, all neatly balled together. My operation begins. I pull apart every pair and then ball the odd ones together. Soon there is a drawer of mismatched socks. Feeling satisfied, I tiptoe back to my room.

The next morning, I wait with bated breath for Jim to lose his temper. Or at least express unhappiness. To my disappointment, there is nothing. He leaves for work in the morning with the usual kiss on Cheryl's cheek and a pat on my head as I eat my cereal. I try to catch a glimpse of his socks, but his trousers go all the way down to his smart office shoes.

Perhaps he has a second sock drawer that I've not discovered.

* * *

All is revealed when he returns home.

Peeping from the top of the stairs, I watch Jim remove his shoes to reveal purple and yellow stripes on his right foot and black and white dots on his left. He must be colour-blind! Or pattern-blind if there is such a thing!

Slipping his feet into his slippers, Jim walks into the kitchen where Cheryl is preparing dinner. I follow closely behind.

"Hello, Ruby," Jim greets me over his shoulder. "Have you had a nice day?"

I shrug. "Spent it reading in the garden."

"Darling, why are you wearing odd socks?" Cheryl asks, staring down at his feet.

"The strangest thing happened, love," Jim replies seriously. "I think the fairies are back."

My head snaps up. What? Fairies? Is he serious?

It seems he is not the only strange one in this house as Cheryl responds, "Really? Again? Gosh, they are a nuisance. What did they do this time?"

"They managed to sneak into my sock drawer and pull every pair apart."

"Such mischief!" Cheryl exclaims.

I can remain quiet no longer. "Fairies? For real?"

The fosters look at me sombrely and nod.

"I'm not six you know," I blurt out. "I'm twelve. Don't talk about fairies for my benefit. I'm not like your other foster children who would have believed it."

"But Ruby," Jim says, "we believe in fairies. There's a whole gang of them in the garden and they're always causing mischief."

"Yeah, OK," I dismiss, standing up. "I'm going to my room."

"But I've made chicken fajitas for dinner," Cheryl protests.

My stomach rumbles at the thought of spicy chicken pieces with salsa, sour cream and salad. I suppress the urge to sit back down to enjoy a plate. "No," I mutter. "I need to be in my room."

OPERATION GLUE

As I lie in bed that night, still a little hungry from only having a cheese sandwich for dinner, it hits me that the fosters are fully aware of what I did with their sock drawer.

The "fairies" nonsense is straight out of the fostering handbook. When children play up, it is advised that attention is diverted, especially for those children that come from family homes like mine.

Fosters are only approved when their evaluation shows that they have a calm temperament. Of course, that wasn't always the case. One foster carer, Steve, had pushed Alisha over when she'd emptied his alcohol bottle down the sink. It was her sixteenth birthday and Steve had offered her wine. Alisha had been furious. "Why can't they read our care plan?" she'd raged. "We are Muslim. We don't drink."

Alisha had rung Poo that very day, and we were back at Sunshine House by nine that night.

What is clear to me now is that Jim is not like horrid Steve. It is going to take a lot to rock his temper.

I pull out my list from under the pillow and switch on my torch, carefully crossing off the first three pranks that are coded pink. I'm going to have to move over to the red side.

The next morning, I wake early to put my plan into action. A few days ago, I'd noticed Jim's toolbox in the cupboard under the stairs and had a quick glimpse inside. It contained just what I needed: a big bottle of PVA glue.

Tiptoeing downstairs, I open the toolbox and pull out the glue tube. Then, moving swiftly, I slather the white goo all over the handles of the doors downstairs.

Ha! Jim will not take too kindly to this.

I don't want to be present when Jim loses his temper, so I remain in my room, standing by the door to hear the outburst that is sure to come from downstairs.

It never comes.

The front door closes at exactly eight o'clock, the time when Jim leaves the house for work. I run to the window overlooking the drive to stare in confusion as a perfectly calm-looking Jim walks to his car. He glances up and catches me staring through the glass. He waves, then gets in and drives off.

I don't understand.

What about the glue? Surely he'd got some on his hands.

"Ruby!" Cheryl calls from downstairs.

I sigh. I may as well have some breakfast as I am famished. I fling open the door and step out into the hallway. Reaching back, I place a hand on the grey metal handle to pull it shut. That is when I feel the gooeyness on my palm.

There is glue all over the handle!

I can't believe it. The fosters have played the prank right back at me. Cheryl must have slathered the glue on when I was at the window. I had been so busy peering at Jim that I hadn't heard any tiny sound from outside the door.

"Ruby!" Cheryl has walked up the stairs and is now standing on the landing . "What are you doing?"

"I uhh…" I don't know what to say.

"What's wrong?" Cheryl asks. "Why are you not letting go of that handle?"

Gosh, Cheryl is a good actress. Fine, I'll play along.

"My hand is stuck."

"What?"

"It's stuck to the handle by some glue or something."

"Oh no," Cheryl cries, rushing forward. "Those awful fairies!"

Fairies! I have to bite my lip to stop the scream. Not that again.

"Here let me help you," Cheryl offers, pulling my hand. It comes unstuck, but not without a slight sting. "You'll have to wash that off with soap. Why don't you do that and then come and have some breakfast?"

I nod, trying to unpick the glue from my palm.

"And then you can help me clean the handles downstairs," Cheryl says. "The fairies have poured glue all over the place. It's a good thing Jim's eyesight is so sharp. He noticed the white goo before he touched it. We've been opening and closing the doors with plastic gloves."

I spend the morning scraping off the glue from the handles. It is not an easy thing to do. By the time I finish, I am determined to finalise Mission Break Up.

Cheryl is preparing dinner when I see my chance. I sneak into Jim's home office to change the Wi-Fi password to AlishaRules!!1.

Ha! The fosters will get increasingly frustrated when their internet won't connect.

Feeling satisfied, I stroll back into the kitchen and ask sweetly, "Can I help?"

Cheryl looks surprised. "Erm, perhaps you could peel those potatoes for me?"

"OK."

When the potatoes are done, Cheryl places lamb joints in two separate trays. "This one's for you," she says, pointing to the smaller one.

The words hit me like a runaway train right in my chest. Why foster me if all they are going to do is make me feel left out? Alisha is right. Fosters only take in kids for the care money they receive. None of them do it out of the goodness of their hearts. None!

"Are you OK?" Cheryl asks in a worried voice.

"My care plan says that I don't eat meat," I snap.

"What?" Cheryl looks taken aback. "You don't eat meat at all?"

"Yes. No. I mean I do," I stutter. "I only eat halal which is the meat that's been blessed with Muslim holy words."

Cheryl blinks and then lets out a nervous laugh. "Oh, I know that! It was in your care plan."

I don't understand. Why doesn't she cook vegetarian food for me like the other fosters did if she knows I can only eat halal meat?

"This here," Cheryl says, lifting the small lamb tray, "is the halal lamb for you. We've got a drawer in the freezer packed with meat and chicken from Khan's Butchers. All the meat dishes I've prepared for you have been halal."

I stare at her. "For real?"

She nods.

"The chicken yesterday was halal?"

"Yes."

I am dumbfounded. Cheryl and Jim had thought of my food requirements to the point where my meat dishes were being prepared separately. No other foster had ever done that before. Well, except one Muslim family who had looked after us during Christmas. They ate halal meat themselves, so they hadn't exactly been going out of their way for us. That stay hadn't lasted beyond the new year. Alisha had hated Saira's house and played a prank with creepy crawlies in a bid to get us kicked out. The sight of three big daddy-long-legs on Saira's pillow was all it had taken to get us kicked out.

Cheryl peers closely at my face. "Is that why you've been insisting on cheese sandwiches on the nights I've cooked meat?"

I nod. "My sister Alisha said I can only eat halal."

"Oh darling!" Cheryl leans over and pulls me into a hug. The move is too sudden, causing me to instinctively push back. She stumbles on her feet a little before recovering. "I'm sorry, I didn't mean to…"

"I'm going to my room," I snap.

The next few hours are spent staring up at the star-covered ceiling. I can't believe the fosters have bought me my own food. It is a kindness that no one else has ever shown. Why can't they be like all the others and just cook vegetarian food for me? Why do they have to treat me in such a nice way? I feel myself warming to them and I do not want that. I want to leave and live with my sister who is my own flesh and blood.

I am still lying on the bed, curled up into a ball, when I hear movement outside the door.

"Ruby," Jim says. "There's a cheese sandwich for you right here, with a glass of milk."

He is home already? What time is it? I glance up at the clock. Dinner time. My stomach rumbles. Another meal of cheese in bread is making me feel queasy. I make up my mind.

Taking a deep breath, I open the door and nearly step onto the food tray. How did I forget that was there! Picking it up, I walk slowly down to the kitchen. Jim and Cheryl are at the dinner table. I catch Cheryl dabbing her left eye with a tissue before they notice me.

Jim shoots to his feet. "Ruby!"

I place the tray on the counter.

"That lamb smells delicious," I say, suddenly feeling very shy. "Could I have the halal one?"

Cheryl's chair scrapes back. "Of course you can. Come, I'll just serve your plate up."

I sit down at the table. It feels strange to be sitting here without Alisha. My sister would have loved the food that Cheryl places in front of me. Roast lamb, potatoes, vegetables and gravy.

"Tuck in," Cheryl says.

I pick up my fork and take a mouthful. It is delicious.

CREEPY CRAWLIES

I feel guilty the next day.

How could I have enjoyed that meal when Alisha is probably living on instant ramen? She used to give me her share of food when I was little. And now here I am eating lamb like a queen.

I also worry about why Alisha hasn't come to see me yet. It's been ten days since our separation and I've not heard a word from her. Poo told her she could call my fosters to arrange a visit to the house. I hope she's alright.

"What would you like to eat today?" Cheryl asks, mid-morning.

"Just a cheese sandwich please," I reply.

Cheryl's face falls, but she doesn't say anything. I retreat into the garden with a book. Being near Cheryl is making me lose focus on my mission. Me and Alisha need each other, and Cheryl and Jim are standing in the way with their do-gooding idea to take care of other people's children.

I slip my Mission Break Up list from between the pages of the book. Operation Sock Drawer, Operation Glue and Operation Wi-Fi have all failed. Last night I enjoyed the meal so much that I'd actually forgotten about the Wi-Fi password change.

It was when we were sitting around the TV that Jim noticed his Wi-Fi wasn't working.

"Did you change the password, dear?" he asked.

Cheryl shook her head, her eyes fixed on the screen.

"Hmm, let me have a look." He disappeared from the room only to return a few minutes later, shaking his head.

"Fairies at it again," he said. "They changed the password to heavens knows what, but I've overridden it. The new password is RubyLivesHere."

"Aww," Cheryl turned away from the TV to smile at me.

I bit my lip to hide my frustration. Well, that was a complete failure of a prank.

"Can I go to my room?" I asked. "I'd like to read in bed and then go to sleep."

"Of course," Cheryl said. "Be sure to brush your teeth. Goodnight!"

That had been last night. Three operations failed. And now what? Perhaps it's time for Operation Creepy Crawlies.

I get to my feet and walk over to the green recycling bin. Lifting the lid, I peer inside. It is full of plastic containers and empty cardboard boxes. Spotting a margarine box, I reach inside to grab it. This will do.

Now what type of insects should I use for my mission? Alisha loved spider pranks, but I can't spot any. I get down on my hands and knees to see if I can spot any worms. None.

Then I see it. A snail slowly creeping along the foot of the fence behind the raspberry bush. I move the branches to peer down. Yes! There are a few of them. Perhaps they are a family. Reaching down, I grab one around the shell and deposit it in the margarine container. Deciding that it needs a friend, I pick up a second one.

"I won't harm you," I whisper. "Just need you both for a mission."

Now I need to figure out where and when to place them to frighten the heebie-jeebies out of Cheryl. Her bed? Hmm, perhaps putting them under the bed covers isn't such a good idea. The snails might suffocate. I don't want that. I know what it is like to be powerless and vulnerable against stronger people.

I make my way to the bathroom. That should be the perfect place as snails like wet surroundings. Yes, I will place them in the bathroom cabinet. I pick up the largest one gently, careful not to hurt it. The perfect spot is right next to Cheryl's face cream. The second snail can go next to the toothbrush holder.

Mission accomplished.

For the rest of the day, I can barely keep the glee off my face.

"You look very happy," Jim comments as we eat a delicious meal of rice and lamb curry.

I nearly choke on my mouthful.

"Just glad to eat food from my culture," I mumble. It isn't a lie, although not the real reason for my joy.

The fosters exchange a look but say nothing.

Bedtime can't come soon enough. Taking my position behind the bedroom door, I listen out for the screams that are sure to come from the bathroom.

At exactly twenty past ten, there is a squeal.

Yes! At last!

Barely able to contain my excitement, I count down from three for the bathroom door to fling open. It is about to happen; Cheryl will run out, terrified, and her screaming will bring the roof down.

I wait and wait.

Nothing.

Exactly seven minutes later, the door creaks open and I hear Cheryl's footsteps on the carpet and then on the stairs. Where is she going? I creep out into the passage to listen out.

Is that... is that the back door being unlocked? Yes! Yes, it is.

Arghh! I want to scream.

Cheryl must be returning the snails to the garden. Apart from the initial squeal, she hasn't freaked out at all. What a waste of a prank.

Shoulders slumped, I drag my feet back to my room and throw myself on the bed. Face down. Is nothing going to work with the fosters?

THE SURPRISE PRANKSTER

I creep down the stairs to the kitchen, early morning. It will be another hour before Jim and Cheryl wake. Taking my time so that I get it right, I stick the duct tape under the sink tap. Jim is always the first one in the kitchen and his routine involves putting the kettle on.

Back in my room. I wait by the door to listen out for his reaction. At exactly ten past seven, I hear him yelling.

Ha!

The duct tape will have caused the tap to spray water in all directions. Judging by the furious reaction, he may well be soaked. My suspicions are confirmed when I catch a glimpse of him through

51

the gap in the door when he comes upstairs. His work suit is wet!

"Fairies again," he says aloud. "We'll have to strike back!"

Strike back?

Good! This pretence can end. They are finally going to ask me to leave.

"What shall we have for dessert?" Cheryl asks after a very tasty meal of Chinese noodles.

Before I can say ice cream, Jim jumps up from the dinner table. "Fly!"

I look around. He must have laser vision because I can't see a thing. "Where?"

Jim stretches his arm up to the ceiling and grabs something in his fist. He opens his palm and I lean over for a glimpse. There's nothing there. I throw a glance at Cheryl by the dishwasher.

"Can I help?" I ask. So far, she hasn't given me any chores, except to keep my bed made and to bring my basket of dirty clothes down every two days.

"No, you're alright," Cheryl says, her head lowered over the arrangement of the crockery.

"Why don't you go through to the living room and I will bring the ice cream when I'm finished here."

Good idea. I scrape back my chair just as Jim launches himself into the air with a tea towel. He just narrowly misses knocking me over.

"Jim!" Cheryl exclaims.

Jim's eyes shine bright and there is excitement on his face. "I've got it."

"Got what?" I demand.

"The fly!" Jim bends down to pick the dead fly off the floor with the tea towel. "Got it!"

I assume he will throw it in the bin. He does no such thing. I watch in horror as he unfolds the tea towel, picks up the black insect and pops it into his mouth.

I want to vomit.

"Ugh!" I gasp in disgust. "You just ate a fly!"

"It's very nice," he says, chewing noisily. "A bit like asparagus."

I am literally gagging. "Ugh! That's sick!"

"Jim!" Cheryl is trying not to laugh.

"You think this is funny?" I shriek. "He just killed and ate a fly."

They both burst out laughing. I don't get it. I stare at them, confused.

"He tricked you," Cheryl says, holding her side as though she has a stitch.

"What?" I don't understand.

"I hid… hid a dry currant in the tea towel and then… then pretended to pick up a fly," Jim explains in between laughing. "It was the currant I ate."

I stare, appalled. "Why would you do that?"

"To play a trick on you," Jim says. "It's no fun if only the fairies have a laugh."

I don't know whether to be offended or amused. It was harmless, and I wasn't affected by the trick directly. I was just grossed out for witnessing what I thought I did. I shrug but can't help the small smile creeping onto my face.

"Oh look! I see it! It's coming!" Jim cries, flinging his tea towel in the air as if it is a victory flag. "She's smiling. We have her first smile."

Cheryl claps her hands. "Yay! You did it, Jim."

I roll my eyes and leave them to their laughter. Honestly, these two treat me like I'm seven years old. I'm still smiling, though, when I pick up the remote control in the living room.

PIZZAGATE

The doorbell rings.

Yes! Mission Break Up is back on and this time will succeed. I am sure of it.

I jump off the sofa, abandoning my favourite Saturday night show to peep around the living room door. Although Jim's frame is obstructing a full view of the visitor, the red cap with the rooster image is still visible, along with the pile of food bags just outside the front door. Ha! It is the delivery guy. He is here to drop off the ten pizzas I ordered online.

"You have the wrong house," Jim argues. "We didn't order them."

"But you did, sir, from your online account with the option to pay cash at the door," the delivery guy insists.

"Let me see the online order," Jim demands

and then turns to shout up the stairs. "Come down, will you, Cheryl."

Jim's shifted position means I have a direct view of the delivery guy. He holds out his phone. "Here you go, sir."

Cheryl comes down the stairs and peers over Jim's shoulder at the receipt.

"I didn't order them," he denies.

"Please." The delivery guy is desperate now. "I won't get paid if you refuse to take them."

Jim and Cheryl exchange a glance. The one that confirms they know I did it.

Yes! Result.

"Well, we don't want that, do we?" Jim's voice changes. He suddenly sounds cheery. "Let's have the boxes then."

"What will we do with them?" Cheryl asks in a worried voice.

"Donate them to the food bank and homeless people," Jim says in the same cheery voice, as if there is nothing more he would like to do on a Saturday night.

"Fabulous idea, darling," agrees Cheryl.

Jim pulls his wallet out from his back pocket. "How much, mate?"

I dart back to the sofa as the delivery guy piles the pizza boxes into the hallway. When Jim and Cheryl walk into the living room, I pretend to be completely engrossed in my TV show.

"Ruby, we need to complete a task and would like you to join us," Jim says.

I pretend it is an effort to tear my gaze away from the screen. "Where do we need to go?"

"To the food bank and the train station," Jim says. "Lots of homeless people gather there at night."

I frown slightly. I don't want to go. I need to distract him. "I suppose you think the fairies ordered the pizzas."

"Oh no, fairies can't communicate," Cheryl says. "We know you did it."

I am still. At last, an acknowledgement of my wrongdoing. It is time for the punishment. Time for them to tell me to leave.

"I didn't realise you had such a gorgeous heart," Cheryl says. "We normally give charity donations from Jim's salary. This will be different."

I am lost for words. They have turned the tables on me again.

"Up you get," Cheryl says.

"But I was going to watch my TV programme," I grumble.

"You can miss this week's episode," Cheryl's voice has an uncharacteristic firmness to it now. "We can't leave you alone in the house and anyway, this is your charitable act. Get your shoes."

Within minutes, I am in the back seat of the car with the pile of pizza boxes beside me. I scowl at everything outside the window as Jim drives us to the centre of town.

The first stop is the food bank, which is next door to the library.

"Just dropping off five boxes of pizza for the volunteers and anyone who comes in tonight," Jim says to the woman in charge. "Courtesy of this little miss."

The woman smiles at me. "What a generous spirit you have."

I gaze down at the floor. Somehow, I don't feel right accepting praise when my intention had nothing to do with being charitable. The woman mistakes it for shyness. "And so sweet."

"Oh, if you only knew," Cheryl says, laughing.

I pick up the double meaning of that line straight away. Cheryl is referring to the pranks I've played. The woman, of course, doesn't know and just beams.

"Right," Jim says. "Now on to the station."

The train station is busy with people coming and going. Some are returning from shopping, others are on their way to central London for a night out. There is an archway on the side and many homeless people gather there.

"Would you like to hand out the boxes?" Cheryl asks me.

"No, I'll do it," Jim interrupts, climbing out of the car. "Everyone has pride, so we're not going to make a fuss and ask for applause. Let me just hand them out and leave."

I stare at the people with their bundles of belongings. Alisha had two older friends who had ended up on the streets after they had left care. Poo was sad about this and said that some people struggled to cope on their own.

"We need to talk," Jim says in a serious voice as he gets back into the car. "It was wrong of you to order the pizzas without our permission. I don't want you to do that again. Is that understood? If you do, then we shall be forced to ground you which means no TV at all."

I bite my lip. Today is another failed result in Mission Break Up.

SWEET BOWL
OF MASH

Cheryl's mum is coming for Sunday lunch.

The fosters announce this to me on Friday. Apparently I have to call her Nana, even though I call Jim or Cheryl by their names. She is not my nana. I have never met my real nana, so I resent having to call a stranger Nana.

When I object, Cheryl explains that her mother thinks of all the foster children in this house as her own grandchildren.

"Would it hurt to make an old lady happy by calling her Nana?" Cheryl asks.

I grudgingly agree.

Better still, I think a prank on Nana will lead to a successful Mission Break Up.

* * *

As I've had no success with Alisha's old pranks, I search the internet for new ones. Luckily, I come across just the right one.

It is lucky that Cheryl is one of those cooks who stores all leftover food in the fridge. Early on Sunday morning before the fosters wake, I open the container of mashed potato and begin re-mashing it until it is as smooth as ice cream.

Then I place it back in the fridge.

My plan is ready.

Nana arrives just after midday in a taxi. She is a small, elderly woman with a kind face. I like her on the spot.

Alisha always taught me to judge people by their expressions. According to her, warm and genuine smiles usually mean that the person is kind.

"Kindness is very important," Alisha used to say, "because the world is very cruel to children without parents."

The reminder of Alisha just brings back the thought that we belong together. We do not have anyone else. Mission Break Up must succeed.

*　*　*

I remain silent throughout lunch. Cheryl and her mum are speaking non-stop to each other. I'm surprised when Jim rolls his eyes at me as if to say "listen to them go on".

After lunch we sit in the living room and I offer to serve the dessert.

"Are you sure?" Cheryl asks, darting a quick look at Jim.

"Yes," I reply sweetly.

In the kitchen, I take out the mashed potato container and scoop it out into a bowl. Then I take the ice cream out of the freezer and serve it in three bowls. The chocolate sauce goes on last.

"Here we are." I place the tray down on the coffee table.

"Such a good helper you have here," Nana says approvingly.

Cheryl makes an odd sound. I can't help wondering if they are onto me.

"Ruby, pass me the remote, please," Jim asks. He is sprawled on his armchair, looking as if he ate one too many Yorkshire puddings.

I turn to the TV stand, pick up the remote and hand it over.

"Thank you."

Bending down, I select the mashed potato bowl and present it to Nana. "For you."

She takes it with a beaming smile. "Thank you, dear."

My own smile is as sweet as the chocolate.

Cheryl and Jim lean forward to take theirs. I pick up the last bowl and sit down. I can't wait for Nana to spit out her mashed potato. Cheryl and Jim are bound to get annoyed. Who knows? They may even lose their tempers.

I watch as Nana pops the spoon in her mouth.

Any minute now and…

There is no reaction, neither negative nor positive. She just carries on eating, as do Cheryl and Jim. Reluctantly, I raise my spoon to my mouth to taste the ice cream.

It is as I suspected. Not ice cream but mashed potato. How could I have mixed up the bowls? How?

Unless… I peep at Jim as he licks his spoon in an exaggerated manner. There is a small smile on his face which I think he is trying to hide. Then it hits me. He switched the bowls when he asked me to pass the remote. How could I have been so dumb?

"Finish your ice cream, Ruby," Cheryl says. "It's really nice."

"Yes, eat up," Jim adds. "Or it will melt."

As if mashed potato can melt!

I manage a small smile and eat.

Mashed potato with chocolate sauce is the most disgusting thing I've ever tasted, but I keep eating until the bowl is clean.

SMASHED SCREEN

This new plan is going to work. It is failsafe.

I have observed that Jim has been working extremely hard on his laptop in the evenings. He says he's putting together a presentation for a new client which will be great for his career.

I am going to break Jim's laptop.

Of course, I'm not really going to do it. I'm just going to let him believe that it is broken. I know not to damage property. Alisha has done it in the past and landed in a lot of trouble. She once smashed a foster's window out of rage. Poo had to use all her charm and contacts to keep the police away.

I don't want that kind of trouble. I just want the fosters to finally let me go. They need to realise that I'm not the one that they can use to play happy families.

***

Back to the plan. I just need to download a screen saver from the internet and apply it. When Jim lifts his laptop lid, his screen will appear smashed, and he will think he can't log on. To his mind, the precious presentation will be gone.

Yes! That is sure to send him over the edge.

I will be thrown out, and then the care money will be allocated to Alisha. We sisters will finally be together.

I lurk around downstairs, waiting for the right time to make my move. I just need to be patient. On Saturday afternoon, he leaves his laptop on the dining table to answer the front door. Seeing my chance, I scoot over to his laptop and download the app.

This is it.

Nothing else has worked.

This must work.

Taking a deep breath, I play the app.

Jim is going to be so mad. I just know it. Feeling a little nervous about the rage that is about to be unleashed, I run up to my room and close the door.

* * *

Exactly eight minutes and twenty-three seconds later.

"Cheryl!"

I nearly jump out of my own skin. That is Jim and he sounds furious.

I run to the door and press my ear against it, expecting more shouting. Nothing. Perhaps he is talking in a low voice, gritting his teeth like I once saw another foster do. It was so intimidating that I'd preferred shouting after that. The thought makes me panic. I need to leave right now. I'm not going to wait for Jim and Cheryl to storm upstairs and talk to me through gritted teeth.

I grab Bug, shove him in a bag and tiptoe downstairs. I can hear low voices in the living room but can't make out the words. I have no intention of trying to figure them out either. Moving as soundlessly as I can, I go through to the kitchen, open the back door and run. I know where Alisha lives. It is time for us to be together.

Almost two hours later, after walking three miles to Alisha's house, I bang on the door until it swings open.

"Hey Ruby," Alisha's housemate greets me. Julie is in full goth attire today.

"Where's my sister?" I demand.

"It's nice to see you too," she says, faking a hurt look.

"Julie!"

"Alright!" She turns away to shout. "Alisha! Look who's here."

Alisha takes her time to appear, and when she finally does, I can't believe how she looks. I have never seen my sister look so scruffy before. Her long hair is a mass of tangles and there are dark circles around her eyes. To make it worse, Alisha's eyebrows are out of shape. I can see stray hairs at the corners. What is going on? Why does she look like this? She doesn't look like she is enjoying life at all.

If I'm shocked at her appearance, then she is just as surprised by mine. The first words she says are, "Your hair!"

I shrug. "I cut it off."

Her mouth falls open and then she recovers, but rather than inviting me in, she rudely asks, "What are you doing here, Rubes?"

"They finally kicked me out," I announce.

Well, that is not entirely true. I ran before they could physically do that.

"Who?"

"The fosters!"

"But why are you here?" Alisha asks in a quiet voice. "Why didn't you call Poo?"

I blink. "Poo? Why would I call Poo?"

"Because she's in charge of you."

"You're in charge of me," I blurt out. "You're my big sister."

Alisha shoves a hand through her tangled hair, suddenly looking very frustrated. "I can't be in charge of you, Rubes."

The lump forms in my throat and I swallow it down quickly. This is not the time to break down. "Why not?"

"Because Alisha doesn't have the money to look after you," Julie says.

"I'm not talking to you," I snap.

She looks offended before stomping back into the house.

"That was really rude," Alisha says.

"I've come to be with you," I say. "Live with you. Remember you promised."

"Yes, one day!" Alisha erupts. "I said that we could live together again one day. But today is not that day. I live in a bedsit. There isn't even space to swing a cat. How am I supposed to take you in?"

"But you said that…"

"One day which is not today!" Alisha shouts.

I stagger back a few steps. Alisha has never shouted at me before. Ever. She always said it was her job as a big sister to look after me. Who is this imposter?

"Look Ruby, you're going to have to return to your fosters," she says. "I can't look after you."

"I'm not going back there."

Something stirs in Alisha's eyes. Is it a hint of the old protection she used to have for me? "Were they mean to you?"

I cannot lie. "No."

I see the relief in her eyes. "Then why can't you go back?"

"I played some pranks, and I don't think they

76

will want me back now."

"They will."

"They won't."

"Then call Poo and tell her to collect you."

I stare at my sister. I can't believe she would rather I was sent back to Sunshine House.

"Alisha…" I plead.

She refuses to listen.

"No, Ruby."

And then to my utter horror, she steps back and slams the door.

Refusing to accept this rejection from my own flesh and blood, I hammer the door with my fist again and again.

"Hey, kid! Enough!" A woman from a top floor window peers out at me.

I scowl. "I need to speak with my sister!"

"Doesn't look like she wants anything to do with you though, does it?"

And that is the truth.

It hits me like a tidal wave.

Alisha does not want me. It is not the case that

she can't have me, it's actually that she's washed her hands of me.

I need to get away from here.

I walk away, blindly. Where can I go? I don't have anywhere to go. I have burned my bridges with the fosters, and I don't have a phone to call Poo. I am homeless, just like all those people at the train station.

I think about going to the train station to join them for the night, but it is too far to walk, and I don't have any money for the bus. As it's a summer's night, I decide to spend the night in the park.

Yes, this is a good plan. I'll make my way to a police station tomorrow where I'll ask them to call Poo. I'm not sure where the station is but I'm sure people will direct me.

The park is near empty except for a group of boys playing football in a far corner. I slump down under a tree and stare up at the changing sky. The blue of the day has given way to orange and red colours, giving it an appearance of flames. The sun disappears slowly off the horizon, just like the hope that I'd had in my heart to be with my sister.

I pull Bug out of the carrier bag to hug him.
I wish my mum were here. The thought of her
releases the tears that I've tried to keep at bay. Not
once did I cry after separating from Alisha, but now
I just can't keep them in. Big fat tears roll down
my cheeks. And for the first time in my life, Alisha
is not with me to wipe them. As my shoulders
heave, it hits me that I have rejected other people's
kindness because I believed Alisha would be there
for me. But she's not.

Jim and Cheryl were so nice to me. Nobody
else had ever bought halal meat for my meals. They
pretended that fairies existed to excuse my pranks,
and they tolerated the unmatched socks, the glue
and the snails.

Fresh tears flow as I realise that I've lost my
only chance of a nice home. I will now spend my
time living in Sunshine House until I'm eighteen.
All alone.

Soon, the boys in the park disappear one by one.
I pull up my knees to my chin and wrap my arms
around my legs. There is a slight chill now and the
trees whisper amongst themselves. When the lamps

glow to their full brightness, I notice a shadow of a man watching me from a distance. I need to keep awake, but I feel so tired. I've walked so much today and then all the crying has completely exhausted me. Perhaps just a little sleep…

"Young lady! Young lady! Wake up!"

I squint against the light of the torch. "What?"

"Ruby Ali?" the voice says.

I scramble to my feet. That is when I realise the two people peering at me are police officers, a man and a woman.

"You're trespassing," the policeman says sternly. "This is a park that closes at nine pm. The caretaker saw you and called it in."

"I was just resting."

"Come on, Ruby." The policewoman's voice is gentle.

"How do you know my name?" I demand.

"Your foster parents reported you missing."

"What? Why?"

"Because they want you back," says the policeman.

ANOTHER MISSION

The front door is yanked open before the police car comes to a halt outside Number 65 Drummond Street.

My stomach flutters nervously when I see Cheryl running down the drive with Jim close behind.

"Out you get, Missy," the policewoman says.

I climb out of the back seat and stand silently on the pavement, eyes down.

"Where did you find her?" Jim demands in a strange, strangled voice.

"Park," the policeman answers. "Caretaker called it in."

"In the park!" Cheryl exclaims. "Oh my goodness, that was so dangerous. Ruby, it was not safe for you to be there at such a late hour. What if something had happened to you? There are all sorts of horrid people who could take advantage of you."

I peep through my lashes. "Sorry."

My words are enough for Cheryl to leap forward and grab me into her arms. At first, I freeze. How can I not? It is a default reaction. I'm not used to being hugged by anyone other than Alisha. Cheryl has grabbed me twice before and both times she sensed my unease and let go. Not this time. Despite standing in her arms like a statue, she refuses to release me. For once I choose not to push her away and, grasping that, she squeezes me even tighter.

"Shall we go inside?" Jim says. His voice seems to have returned to its normal pitch. "It's rather dark out here."

Cheryl finally lets me go and stands with her arm around my shoulders. I can't bring myself to look up at him. I think he senses my discomfort because he says, "It's OK, Ruby, the fairies failed to break my laptop. They downloaded a prank app."

That untimely, annoying lump is back in my throat again. I swallow hard and nod.

"After you," the policeman says.

We walk inside to sit in the living room.

"Poonam is on her way," Cheryl says. "I rang her as soon as we got the call that you've been found."

The policeman looks down at me. "Why did you run away from home?"

"I went to see my big sister…" my voice trails off.

"And?" the policeman wants to know.

I shrug. I don't want to say it aloud that Alisha rejected me. If I do that, then I'll l be admitting that I'm all alone in the world.

The doorbell saves me from any more questions from the police. Poo is here. Well, even if I never have anyone else in the world again, I know I'll always have Poo. The sudden realisation makes me feel a burst of warmth for Poo. She is the one person who has remained constant in our lives. Right from the very first time when she gathered me in her arms and walked out of the flat that smelled of death.

Before the police had found us, Alisha and I had been hungry for days. A neighbour had finally heard Alisha's banging on the locked front door and raised the alarm. Poo had been the first one there with the police. And here she is again, in her blue flowery dress over a pair of skinny jeans and blue converse.

"Hello, Ruby."

"Hello, Poo," I reply.

I can't help feeling a little bad. I know she has children of her own, and she's had to leave them to rush here in the night.

"Right, well, why don't we all go in the kitchen and have a cup of tea," the policewoman suggests.

I get up, suddenly feeling famished. I have not eaten since breakfast.

"Not you," the policewoman says. "You and your social worker need to talk."

I sit back down as the others leave.

Poo stands by the window. "Are you OK?"

I nod.

"Where did you go before you were found at the park?"

"To Alisha's house," I answer.

"Why?"

"To be with her."

"So how did you end up in the park?"

Poo is going to make me say it. I take a deep breath and rush the words out. "Because she didn't want me."

"How did that make you feel?"

Upset. Terrified. Abandoned.

I choose a less loaded word. "Alone."

"But you're not alone, are you, Ruby?" Poo says. "Cheryl and Jim are very good foster parents, aren't they?"

I cannot deny it. "Yes. They are the best."

Poo sits down on the sofa next to me. "What am I going to do with you?"

I shrug.

"Do you still want to live with Alisha?"

I shrug again, trying not to look like it bothers me, but I am sure the tremble in my voice gives me away. "She slammed the door in my face."

"Oh baby." Poo leans over and gathers me in her arms.

For the second time tonight, I don't push the other person away. "Do you think Cheryl and Jim still want me?" I whisper.

Poo leans back and takes hold of my face between her two hands. I want to look away, but Poo's grip is firm.

"Cheryl and Jim love having you here," she says. "They want to provide a home for you. Can't you see that?"

I realise it then. The fairies were all about making this house my home.

"I would really like to stay here," I admit.

Poo lets go of my face. I watch as she pulls her phone out of her bag.

"They're only in the kitchen," I say. "I could just call the fosters and the police."

"Not them I'm calling." Poo presses a button and when the call is answered, says, "Come through the front door, I've left it ajar."

Who is Poo talking to? I see for myself when Alisha steps into the living room.

"Hey Rubes."

My heart hammers in my chest. I'm not sure that I want to see or speak to my big sister just yet. I sink back into the sofa.

"Sulking with me, are you?" Alisha says lightly.

"No," I deny.

"I'm sorry about earlier," she says.

I shrug, avoiding her eyes.

"So, this looks like a nice place," Alisha says, trying to make conversation. "Poo said they even make halal meals for you. You're lucky."

I refuse to respond, and the room soon fills with an awkward silence.

It is Poo who finally breaks it. "How's the world treating you, Alisha?"

"Harder than I thought it would be," she automatically replies.

"Did you hear that, Ruby?" Poo says. "Alisha's finding it hard to make her way in the world. She has a job as a waitress, and she works really hard, long into the night. She lives in a bedsit which is all she can afford. Don't you want her to build her life up properly first?"

I shrug again.

"Well, then let her go," Poo says gently. "Don't make her feel guilty about trying to live her life."

"But…" I protest. When did I try to make Alisha feel guilty?

"Alisha rang me in tears after your visit," Poo says. "She felt bad for turning you away. She wanted me to explain how hard it would be for her to look after you."

I look up at Alisha. She cried? My big sister never cries.

"Rubes, I will always be your big sister," Alisha says. "Always. You'll never be alone."

"You'll always be my big sister?" I repeat in a trembling voice.

"How can you even ask that?" Alisha demands, dragging me into her arms for a tight hug. "Always. We're flesh and blood."

I hug Alisha back. I wish I didn't have to let go, but I know now that I must. She needs to build her life, just like I will when I turn eighteen.

"I love you," I say when we step back from each other.

"I love you too, Rubes," Alisha responds.

Poo gets to her feet. "Right, that's settled then. Ruby, call the others."

I pop my head out of the door. "Cheryl, Jim?"

The four adults walk back in.

The policeman looks around. "How are we doing then?"

"We're all good," Poo replies, "This is Alisha, by the way. Ruby's big sister."

Alisha raises a hand in greeting.

The officers nod and then turn to leave. "We'll be off then."

"Bye and thank you," I suddenly blurt.

They look at me in surprise and then the policewoman beams. "You're very welcome. Stay safe."

And then they are gone.

"Alisha," Cheryl suddenly says as Poo and Alisha get ready to leave. "Would you like to come for Sunday lunch? I'm roasting a halal chicken for Ruby and I think it'll be too big for her to finish."

Alisha's eyes look a bit moist, but then she blinks, and they are dry again. "I would love that. Thank you."

"Lunch is at one thirty. See you then."

Poo pats Cheryl's back. "You're one of the good eggs. See ya."

Alisha hugs me by the door. "You'll be alright, kid. I promise. The fosters seem really nice, and I'll try to come and see you when I can."

"You promise to come on Sunday?"

"I won't miss it for the world," Alisha reassures. "I'm so bored of ramen."

"I've been feeling really guilty about all the nice meals because you're missing out," I admit.

Alisha sighs. "Stop doing that. I am living my life and you need to live yours."

I nod and she gives me one last quick hug before disappearing through the door. Then it is just me and the fosters again.

I run a hand through my untidy hair. "Could you take me to your hairdresser soon?" I ask shyly. "My hair could do with a trim."

Cheryl looks like she will burst with happiness. She nods enthusiastically.

"Are you hungry?" Jim asks, putting an arm around Cheryl.

"So much," I admit.

"Well let's get you a glass of milk and some food," he says.

I follow the fosters into the kitchen and sit down at the table. There is a warm feeling inside me, and I embrace it. It is new and it is all because I finally know that I'm not alone. I never have been. Alisha will always be there. So will Poo. And I am living with the nicest fosters. Who knows? Perhaps they will let me stay until I turn eighteen.

READING ZONE!

QUIZ TIME

Can you remember the answers
to these questions?

· Why is Alisha no longer allowed to
be in care with Ruby?

· What was the last thing that Ruby's
mum gave to her?

· What is Ruby expecting Jim to do when
he finds all his odd socks?

· Why does Ruby play so many pranks
on the fosters?

· How did the police officers know
Ruby's name?

READING ZONE!

GET CREATIVE

Ruby and Alisha have played lots of pranks on their different foster parents. Have you ever played a prank on anyone? Has it worked or did it backfire?

Choose a prank from the book or think of your own. Write a set of instructions to show someone else how to play the same prank. Can you think of some ways to ensure the prank doesn't backfire?

READING ZONE!

STORYTELLING TOOLKIT

The author does not start the book by telling us why Ruby and Alisha are in care. As the story moves on, we find out details about them. These details give us a clear picture of Ruby and Alisha's life and add to our emotions at the end of the story.

This is a good skill to use in your own writing: feed the details of characters to your reader throughout the story rather than giving everything away in the first paragraph.